DORY
FaNTaSMaGory
Head in the Clouds

ABBY HANLON

PUFFIN BOOKS

For Ivah, Alexandra, and Henry

PUFFIN BOOKS
An imprint of Penguin Random House LLC
375 Hudson Street
New York, New York 10014

First published in the United States of America by Dial Books for Young Readers,
an imprint of Penguin Random House LLC, 2018
Published by Puffin Books, an imprint of Penguin Random House LLC, 2019

Visit us online at penguinrandomhouse.com

THE LIBRARY OF CONGRESS HAS CATALOGED THE DIAL EDITION AS FOLLOWS:
| Names: Hanlon, Abby, author. |
Title: Head in the clouds / Abby Hanlon. |
Description: New York, NY : Dial Books for Young Readers, [2018]
| Series: Dory Fantasmagory ; 4 | Summary: Dory, nicknamed Rascal, has her first
loose tooth, but her excitement turns to concern when imaginary evil robber
Mrs. Gobble Gracker captures the tooth fairy.
Identifiers: LCCN 2017043440 | ISBN 9780735230460 (hardback) Subjects: | CYAC: Teeth—
Fiction. | Tooth Fairy—Fiction. | Imagination—Fiction. | Brothers and sisters—Fiction. | Family
life—Fiction. | BISAC: JUVENILE FICTION / Readers / Chapter Books. | JUVENILE FICTION /
Imagination & Play. | JUVENILE FICTION / Humorous Stories.
Classification: LCC PZ7.H196359 He 2018 | DDC [Fic]—dc23
LC record available at https://lccn.loc.gov/2017043440

Puffin Books ISBN 9780735230477

Printed in the United States of America
Designed by Jennifer Kelly

1 3 5 7 9 10 8 6 4 2

HEAD IN THE CLOUDS

If your head is in the clouds,
it means your thoughts are far away
and you are in your own world,
daydreaming or living in a fantasy.

CHAPTER 1
Such a Bunchy Coat

My name is Dory, but most people call me Rascal. I have an enemy named Mrs. Gobble Gracker—you might have heard of her. She has been trying to catch me and bring me to her cave. But today I have a problem that's even bigger than Mrs. Gobble Gracker. It's this coat.

My mom says, "Oh! I just can't stand how cute it is. It's adorable on you."

"It's bunchy," I say.

"It's nice and cozy," she says.

"It's all puffed up and bunchy!" I cry.

"It's a fabulous coat," she says, kissing me.

"Someone put pillows in it. That's why it's all BUNCHY! I'm not wearing it!"

"Oh, stop," says my mom. "You are wearing it, Rascal. No matter what. It's freezing out."

"PILLOWS! Bunchy pillows!"

"Stop saying pillows. You're wearing it."

"You always make me wear bunchy pillows!!"

"Come on, fluffball," says my big brother, Luke. "We're leaving."

And stop saying bunchy!

"Hey, that used to be my coat," says my big sister, Violet. "But I'm pretty sure it looked *a lot* better on me."

Great coat, kid!

When I get to school, I see my friends Rosabelle and George in the school yard. As soon as I see them, I take off my coat. "Nobody!—and I mean NOBODY!—can make ME wear this Ugly Garbage Bunchy Pillow Coat!!!!!!"

"Okay," shrugs George. "Raise your hand if you want to play hamsters."

But right in the middle of our game, it's time to go inside.

"Dory, you're going to remember our morning routine today, *right*?" asks my teacher.

4. Raise your hand and wait for your math to be checked.

5. Read quietly on the rug until morning meeting.

6. Be a good listener during morning meeting.

When it's time to line up for lunch and recess, everybody goes to the closet to get their coats.

I walk to the closet, too, but when I see my bunchy coat on the floor ... my arm won't bend.

So I line up without the coat. *It's not cold out.*
My teacher won't even notice.

"I still hear talking," says the teacher. "When
I have a quiet line, we'll go . . . wait . . . what's
this?" She picks up the bunchy pillow coat
from the closet floor.

"Whose is this?"

I'm about to say, "It's mine," but now . . . my mouth won't open.

"Everybody look up here, please. Does anyone know whose coat this is?"

Rosabelle is about to say my name, but then she sees my face. She seals her lips shut. Tight.

mouth won't open

"I know this coat must belong to somebody. It didn't just magically appear in this classroom."

George is looking at me, too. His eyes are bulging out of his face.

I look down at my sneakers.

"Dory . . . you're not wearing a coat. Isn't this yours?"

My head shakes itself.

I didn't tell it to, but it does anyway! First my arm, then my mouth, now my head! Are my body parts under some kind of spell?

head shakes itself

Now everyone is looking at me, not just Rosabelle and George.

"Are you sure?" asks my teacher.

"Yes," I lie.

"Dory, are you saying your mom sent you *without* a coat?"

"Uh-huh."

"On this freezing cold day?"

"Uh-huh."

"Hmmmmmm. Well, then you can borrow this one," she says.

Okay.

Then I realize—*it must be the coat that has put a spell on me. An evil spell that made me lie!* Now I really HAVE TO get rid of it!

So . . . after we eat lunch and everybody is putting their coat on, I leave the coat on the bench *by mistake* and run out to play.

In the school yard, I run around so fast that nobody notices I'm not wearing a coat.

But as soon as I walk into the classroom, the teacher says, "Dory, where's that coat you borrowed?"

Uh-oh. If I don't lie now, she'll know I was lying before. "Ummm . . . I put it in my back-pack. In the closet," I lie.

"Wait. So it *was* yours?"

"Yeah . . . I . . . uh . . . just forgot how it looked cause . . . sometimes it looks . . . bunchy," I lie.

"I knew it had to be yours! But when did you put it in the closet?" She looks super-duper confused.

"Uhhhh . . . when I was . . . was . . . going to the bathroom," I lie.

"Hmmm, okay," says my teacher. Then she turns her head away from me.

I walk back to my desk thinking, *I did it!* I got away from the evil coat. I imagine the coat blowing away, up to the clouds, gone forever.

But then Benji, who works in the cafeteria, comes into our classroom during writing time ...

AND HE'S
HOLDING THE
COAT!!!!!

"Hey, kids! This coat was left in the cafeteria. Does this belong to anyone in here? Before I take it to the lost and found ... I mean, *what a good-looking coat!*"

My teacher's head turns very quickly to look at me. Now she doesn't look super-duper confused anymore. She looks like she's going crazy! "Dory . . . I thought you just said your coat was in your backpack. Isn't this your coat?" asks my teacher.

I slip down low in my chair.

Nope.

"Didn't you say . . . wait a minute . . . Go show me the coat in your backpack. And please ask your mom to label your coat!"

I walk slowly to the closet.

"Alrighty, kiddos, I hate to bring such a *snazzy coat* to the lost and found, but that's where it will be," says Benji.

I don't know what to do when I get to the closet. I don't even have my backpack! I stand in the closet. Deep in a corner. How do I break this evil spell? Do you get in trouble if you tell on yourself? I wonder.

"Rascal, come out. The teacher forgot all about you!" It's George.

"How come?"

"Because Charlie threw up in the water fountain!"

"He did?"

"And he gets to go home!" George says.

"No fair!" I say. I hand Charlie his backpack since I'm in the closet anyway.

When I come out of the closet, I see that George was right.

She definitely forgot about me!

At the end of the day, my mom picks me up in the school yard. She says, "Rascal, where on earth is your coat? It's freezing out!"

"Yes, I would really like to talk to you about that," says my teacher who did *not forget*.

I slowly walk backward away from them. Then I watch from far away. My teacher keeps talking and talking and talking. Her hands move around a lot. My mom is surprised.

As I watch my mom's face, I start crying because I know I'm in really big trouble.

Finally, my mom walks over to me. "Come on," she says in an angry voice. "We are going to the lost and found."

We don't have to look deep in the bin, because the coat is right on top. She hands it to me and I put it on.

"How many lies did you tell today, Rascal?"

I try and count on my fingers. "One . . . two . . . three . . . seven, I think. Or maybe eight?" A hundred tears run down my face.

"Oh boy," she says. "You are in really big trouble."

Then she looks up at the sky and whispers, "Oh, why, why, why, why?" She takes a long breath. When she's done breathing, I ask her, "Do I have to wear this coat again?"

"No, you don't," she says.

I wipe my tears and smile. I love my mom so much. I hug her leg so tight that she can't shake me off. My body is stuck to her leg. I think it must be the spell.

Oh, this child.

CHAPTER 2
Sticky Licorice

When we get home, my mom says that I have to write an apology letter to my teacher.

"A letter? That's it?!" asks Luke.

"Yeah! I would have been grounded for a month if I lied to my teacher!" says Violet.

"Rascal is always going to be bad . . . if all she has to do is write a letter!" says Luke.

"She's not bad, she just made a mistake," says my mom. "Well . . . several mistakes."

"You're bad!" Luke says to me.

"Bad to the bone," says Violet.

"That's enough," says my mom. She picks me up and carries me away from them.

"It was an evil spell," I whisper back at them. "The coat put an evil spell on me."

But this makes them even angrier.

"Just because you have a stupid imagination . . ." says Luke.

". . . doesn't mean you can get away with everything!" says Violet.

"Can my punishment be time-out instead?"
I ask my mom. If I had time-out, I could play
with Mary in my room.

"First write the letter," she says.

I stare at the blank piece of paper for a long
time.

Then I ask my mom, "How do you spell 'sorry'?"

"S-O-R-R-Y," says my mom, looking pleased.

"How do you spell 'bunchy'?" I ask.

She sighs. Then she says, "B-U-N-C-H-Y."

"How do you spell 'world of danger'?"

"W-O-R-L... you know what... just sound it out." She leaves the room and I keep writing.

"How do you spell 'meat loaf'?" I call to her.

"Huh? What are you writing?" she calls back.

"Sound it out!" she yells.

"How do you spell 'five little ducklings'?"

"What on earth?" says my mom, walking back into the kitchen.

"How do you spell 'electric can opener'? How do you spell 'cemetery'?"

"Rascal, shush! Listen to me. What is the important thing that you need to say in this letter?"

"That I'll never lie again—cross my heart, hope to die, stick a needle in my eye."

"Okay, so did you write that?" she asks.

"No, that happens at the end. When I'm riding a powerful black horse. And all the animals cheer. And there's a sunset."

"Okay, let's just skip to that part," she says. "I'll help you."

Finally, I'm done. My mom puts my letter in an envelope, and I run up the stairs to my room as fast as I can.

But when I open
my door, the first
thing I see are these:

Then this:

And then this:

"What the heck!?" I yell at Mary. "What is Mrs. Gobble Gracker doing here?"

"She rang the doorbell in her bathrobe. She said she's sick! I felt so bad, I didn't know what to do. She said she had no one to take care of her," says Mary.

"She's not sick! She's faking! It's a trick! Haven't you ever read Little Red Riding Hood? She's the wolf! Look at her! She's lying!"

"I'd love some hot coffee," croaks Mrs. Gobble Gracker in a fake-sick voice.

"This is ridiculous!" I shout at Mary.

"And I wouldn't say no to some soup," says Mrs. Gobble Gracker.

"Mary! I have had A VERY HARD DAY! AND NOW THIS? You get her out of here right now!"

"But how? Wait . . . where are you going?"

"Somewhere safe! Out of this house!" I say. I grab the first thing I see—my goggles—and run downstairs to find my mom. "Be careful she doesn't eat you!" I call back to Mary. "HIGH DANGER ALERT!"

"It's not safe for me to stay in this house," I tell my mom.

Can we go to the pool?

"Not today," she says.

"How come?"

"'Cause it's winter," she says, "and the pool is outside. Remember?"

"You always say no. Can we go to the post office then?"

"What? No."

"How about the library? The hardware store? Don't we usually have errands? Or remember that time we went to the shoe repair? Can we go there again? I know! How about *you* get your hair cut? Don't you like doing that? And remember that time when I went with you? And everyone said how *good* I was. All the hair ladies were saying it!"

"We are staying home," says my mom. "And guess what! Melody and her mom are coming over."

"Melody is coming over?! *Why!!!*" Melody lives on my block. Her mom is friends with my mom. She cries about everything. She even cried one time because her straw bent.

And she always wants to clean things. One time, she spent the whole playdate vacuuming.

Ding-dong!

"Who's that?"

"Oh, great, they're here," says my mom. "Go answer the door. And take your goggles off."

Melody's mom says quietly to me, "Melody is a little scared of your game about that evil witch . . . Mrs. What-was-it?"

"Gobble Gracker."

"Yes. . . . So could you maybe . . . not talk about her . . . and try and play something else?"

"Like what?" I say in a grumpy voice.

"Like a board game," says my mom.

"Oh hey, kids, Melody is here," says my mom to Luke and Violet as they are coming downstairs. When they hear Melody's name, they quickly turn around and run back up-stairs as fast they can.

My mom gives me a look like I better behave.

"Wanna play Candy Land?" I ask Melody.

"I guess so," she says.

The moms go into the kitchen to have tea.

I let Melody go first. Luckily, she keeps getting double color cards, so she's ahead of me on the path. I cross my fingers behind my back that she wins because I don't want her to cry. I'm secretly happy when I get a green card, which means I get stuck in a licorice space.

But she starts crying anyway!

"No! I'M stuck in the sticky licorice!" I say. "Not you. See, I'm red! You're yellow."

"I know."

← me

Licorice

"So why are you crying?"

"'Cause I feel bad for you," she says, crying.

I always think she's fake crying because of the things she cries about . . . BUT THEN right after I'm positive that she's faking, these ENORMOUS tears spill out of her eyes. Tears so big that the board gets wet!

"No, it's okay! I just miss one turn. I don't mind. It's no big deal," I tell her.

"Can we clean it up?" asks Melody.

"Clean up the licorice? That's a great idea!"

"No, I meant the game," she says.

"The licorice is a sticky mess! It's all over the floor! Come on," I say. "Get up!"

The licorice is spreading all over Candy Land! We've got to clean it up to save Candy Land!

We run to the bathroom and grab a pile of rags and a bottle of soap. Suddenly Melody is not quiet at all anymore. "Turn on the shower!" yells Melody. "It will wash the licorice away!"

Then she starts scrubbing the hallway.

Excuse me. It's not safe in here for playdates.

The licorice IS EVERY-WHERE!

MORE SOAP!

I think it was the goggles that made it hard to see after they got foggy from the shower.

And I guess the floors were pretty slippery, too.

Because when Melody and I crashed into each other, I landed right on top of her and her foot went into my mouth.

"Are you okay?" Melody asks. I take off my goggles.

"Something is wiggling in my mouth," I say.

"It's your tongue," says Melody.

"No, it's something else," I say. I put my hand in my mouth to feel. "My loof is toof," I say. "I mean, my toof is loof."

"Let me feel," says Melody. She wiggles my tooth.

"Yup, it wiggles!" she whispers.

"My first loose tooth!!!!" I yell.

And then Melody bursts into tears. The giant kind.

"Oh no! Why are you crying!"

"Do you know what this means?" she asks.

"Yes! It means the tooth fairy is coming!!"

"It means you are growing up!" she sobs.

"It's okay." I hug Melody. "I'll always be a baby."

CHAPTER 3
Baby Teeth

"HOLY COW. My wiggly tooth is so wiggly!" I tell Luke and Violet that night before bed. "MY WIGGLY TOOTH IS SO WIGGLY!"

"You said that already," says Luke.

"I just want to make sure the tooth fairy hears," I say. "I think the tooth fairy is a sparkly little glow of light. And she lives on a fluffy cloud. And she is so little that she could fit in my pocket . . . she has soft fuzzy wings . . . and she's a zippy little flier!"

"Do you think she'll bring me a dollar?" I ask
Luke and Violet. "Does she know me already?
Does she love me so much? Because I love her!
I love her more than anything, even candy!"

"If you don't stop talking
about love, I will pull your tooth
out right now," says Luke.

"And it will be very bloody," says Violet.

I don't know why Luke and Violet are so mean to me, but I think it has something to do with their memories.

"Didn't Mom tell you to go to bed a long time ago?" asks Luke, giving me a kick off the couch.

"There's a problem with my bed," I tell them.

"What kind of problem?" asks Violet.

"Mrs. Gobble Gracker is in my bed," I whisper.

"MMMMMOOOOOMMMM!" yells Violet. "Rascal is talking about Mrs. Gobble Gracker again!"

My mom and dad come out of the kitchen. "Come on, Rascal! It's bedtime. You know that," says my mom.

"But Mrs. Gobble Gracker is in my bed!" I cry.

"No more games tonight. It's over," says my mom. "I'm done."

"And she wants to butter my bones!"

"What does that mean exactly?" asks Luke.

"Butter my bones . . . and EAT them!!!" I yell.

"*Crunch, crunch*," says Violet, pretending to eat my arm. "Deee-licious!"

"Let's go," says my mom. "Daddy will read you a story."

"Mrs. Gobble Gracker can listen, too," says my dad. "She can even pick the book."

Mrs. Gobble Gracker is a terrible listener.

When my dad turns out the light he says, "Think happy thoughts, Rascal."

"Like what?" I ask him.

"How about . . . the tooth fairy! If you think about the tooth fairy, I bet Mrs. Gobble Gracker will go away." He kisses me good night and leaves me alone with Mrs. Gobble Gracker.

"WHO is the tooth fairy?!" I say, and turn

on the light. "You have been alive for 507 years and you've never heard of the tooth fairy!"

"Just tell me," she says.

So I explain it to her. Of course, she interrupts. "So are you trying to tell me that there is a woman—not me—who sneaks into children's rooms in the middle of the night without permission and takes their body parts? And it's not me?"

"Just teeth! That's the only body part," I say. "Teeth that already fell out."

"From eating too much candy?" she asks.

"Not rotten teeth! Baby teeth!" I say.

"*Baby teeth?*" And then she sits up in bed and starts talking in a high baby voice. "That sounds so cute! Oh yes, yes! Little mini–baby teeth! I want them. I want them!"

"What?"

"Oh, nothing. Forget it. And so tell me again . . . children *want* her to come? And they are *happy* about it? And she never gets in trouble for doing this?"

"Yeah, 'cause she gives them money. . . . Why are you asking? What are you thinking?"

"Oh, me? Nothing. I'm not thinking of anything perfectly evil," she says, getting out of bed.

Then Mrs. Gobble Gracker starts pulling things out of my closet and making a huge mess.

"Do you have any wings?" she asks. "You know, from a Halloween costume or something."

"Nope."

"How about a little crown? You must have a crown!"

"I don't."

"EVERY GIRL GOES THROUGH A PRINCESS PHASE—WHERE ARE THE CROWNS!?!?"

"Why are you yelling? Calm down," I say.

"Okay, just tell me . . . do you have glitter? Your mom probably hides it from you because you always make a huge mess with it. Maybe in a kitchen cabinet? I must have glitter! I CAN'T DO THIS WITHOUT GLITTER!"

She runs downstairs. I hear some noise in the kitchen and then the sound of the front door slamming. She's gone. I guess my dad was right.

I fall asleep with a happy thought.

CHAPTER 4
Cooked Eggs

When it's time to leave for school in the morning, my mom gives me Luke's old coat. "Here, you can wear this beat-up old coat," she says.

I love this coat! It's not bunchy. And it doesn't have pillows in it. *It's flat.* I wiggle my fingers in the soft furry pockets.

And guess what I find?

"Look! I found a mini–candy cane!"

"Well, that's mine then," says Luke.

"Nope, it's in my coat now, so it's MINE."

"No it's not! Give it to me, Rascal!"

The wrapper is melted and stuck all the way around the candy cane. I won't have time to unstick the wrapper before Luke tackles me. So as fast as I can, I stuff the whole thing in my mouth and start chewing.

I close my eyes . . . and I'm far away in Candy Land—deep in the Peppermint Forest.

"SHE'S EATING THE WRAPPER!" yells Luke.

Chew, chew, gulp.

"What wrapper?" calls my mom.

"The candy cane wrapper!" yells Violet.

Chew, chew, gulp.

"Candy cane? Where did you get candy canes from?" asks my mom.

"Rascal, did you eat the wrapper?" asks my mom.

I look at Luke and Violet. I look at my mom. I make a very bad decision.

"No," I lie.

We wait to see whose side my mom is going to take.

"If she ate the wrapper, I think she'll be okay. We don't have time for more fighting. You're going to be late for school."

"But it was MY CANDY CANE!" yells Luke. "And she lied!!"

"Don't worry," Violet says to Luke. "We don't need Mom's help. It's time WE took matters into our own hands."

For most of the way, Luke and Violet walk in front of me, but I keep talking anyway.

Then Luke and Violet wait
for me to catch up.

"So, Rascal, we were wondering . . . did
Mom and Dad ever tell you the whole story
about the tooth fairy?" asks Violet.

"What do you mean?" I ask.

"Well, if they didn't tell you, maybe we
shouldn't," says Violet.

"No, tell me! Please!"

"'Cause they probably don't want you to be
too curious," says Violet.

70

"I won't be curious," I say. "Tell me!"

"Only if you promise not to tell Mom and Dad that we told you."

"I promise," I say. "I won't tell."

"Okay, well . . . for one thing, the tooth fairy isn't little," says Violet. "She's regular size."

"A regular-size fairy like Mr. Nuggy? Wow!" I say.

"And she doesn't even wear wings . . ." says Violet.

"Why not?"

"I don't know, but—"

"I know! Maybe she thinks the wings are too itchy. Maybe she hates them so she only wears them when she has to," I say.

"The thing is," says Violet, "she is a pretty cranky lady. She's not all cute and lovey-dovey. She's more like . . . hhhhmmmm, how do I say this? . . . *a serious grouch.*"

"Yeah!" I say. "Because being the tooth fairy is a really hard job. She's so busy every night and she doesn't get a lot of sleep, so she's overtired. She gets so sweaty flying around all night, so sometimes she just wears a bathing suit and then if she flies over a swimming pool, she can take a quick break and . . ."

"Ah-hum! As I was saying—" says Violet.

"And I bet she has a giant purse," I say, "and it's a huge mess inside! It's full of teeth and money, and she never remembers to throw her garbage away, and she secretly eats a lot of candy . . . and OF COURSE she doesn't wear

wings because she doesn't wear a crown, either! Because she doesn't want everyone to know who she is!!! 'Cause she's more like a spy! Yeah! SHE HAS A SPY HAT! And I bet her bathing suit is glow-in-the-dark!"

"Fine, she wears a bathing suit, whatever, Rascal. But there's one more thing I have to tell you about the tooth fairy."

"I know! I know what it is! She's getting a divorce!"

"What? No."

"Then what?"

"Well . . . she cares A LOT about behavior. So, if you're bad, she doesn't give you money."

I stop walking.

"The tooth fairy doesn't care if you're bad. That's Santa!" I say.

"They're friends!" says Luke.

"And she's the one who gave Santa the idea in the first place," says Violet.

"So then what happens?" I ask. "I mean, if you're bad? What does she bring instead?"

"Well, it never happened to us." Violet shrugs. "'Cause we're good. So we're not sure. But it would probably be something you really hate."

"Like what?" I ask.

Then Luke, who has been quiet for a long time, suddenly bursts out, "I know what it is! It's eggs! She brings you eggs!"

"Eggs? That's the Easter Bunny!" I say.

"Not chocolate eggs!" he says, and then he smiles. "Cooked eggs!"

"So you mean . . . like an omelet?" I ask him.

"Possibly," says Luke.

"I *hate omelets!*"

"So . . . then an omelet would be *very likely,*" he says, nodding his head a lot. "She can just slide it under your pillow."

"Well, I am not bad," I say. "So I don't care. I DON'T CARE ONE TINY STUPID BIT," I shout, and kick a bunch of dirt. But secretly, I'm worried. Very worried. If I had a banana right now I would call my fairy godmother, Mr. Nuggy. Because I think this is an emergency.

When I get to school, I give my letter to the teacher.

She says, "Thank you for the letter, Dory. But instead of going out to play for recess today, you will stay in the classroom. Because you didn't tell the truth yesterday, I need you to spend some quiet time thinking about your behavior."

NO RECESS?

Last year Jane missed recess because she bit Pablo's arm when he wouldn't hold her hand when they were line partners because he said she had cream cheese on her hand. And once Pablo missed recess because he kicked George in the butt, but Pablo said it wasn't his fault because George begged him to.

I've never missed recess.

Bad kids miss recess.

Now I think Violet was right—I am bad. *Bad to the bone.*

I don't start crying until lunchtime. Because everybody knows what comes after lunch.

"We won't play hamsters at recess without you," says George. "We promise."

"Is Mrs. Gobble Gracker back? Is that why you are crying? Are you in danger?" asks Rosabelle.

"She's crying so hard that I can't understand her," says George.

"Wait … listen … I think she said something about the tooth fairy," says Rosabelle.

"The tooth fairy? Why is she crying about the tooth fairy?" asks George.

"Oh my goodness! Is the tooth fairy missing?" asks Rosabelle. "Or did she get hurt? Did she fly into a building? Did she fall off a cloud? Did she slip in the bathtub?"

"Don't tell me she choked on a hot dog!" says George.

"Well, good thing none of us has a loose tooth right now!" says Rosabelle.

I show them my wiggly tooth.

Then my teacher taps me on the shoulder and says, "Pack up your lunch box. It's time for you to come with me." She's eating a banana!

I'm not going to do anything crazy—like ask my teacher if I can make a phone call from her banana or anything.

But I want to.

Without the kids, the classroom looks big and empty. My teacher says I can read books on the rug. But I sit by the window and watch the clouds float by instead. My teacher eats her lunch and checks our homework.

And then a fluffy cloud floats by . . . with someone on it.

"So, what do you think of my new look?" yells Mrs. Gobble Gracker.

"I think you look kinda dumb," I say.

"Excuse me! Is that any way to talk to the tooth fairy?" she says. "By the way, my wings don't actually work. They're just costume wings."

"You can't just dress up and say you're the tooth fairy. That's not how it works. There's only one tooth fairy in the world," I tell her.

"*Only one?*" she asks.

Suddenly, Mrs. Gobble Gracker is in a big rush. She gets in a little airplane and swoops by the window and out of sight.

Mrs. Gobble Gracker is definitely up to something, but I can't stop worrying about omelets. I try not to wiggle my tooth, but I can't stop that either.

CHAPTER 5
Nighty-Night

After school, I run into the house so I can FINALLY call Mr. Nuggy. I slide across the kitchen floor in my socks, heading straight for the fruit bowl. And then I discover something terrible.

We have no bananas.

I think about having a temper tantrum—
just a mini one. Luke and Violet are not happy,
either.

"I didn't have time to go grocery shopping
today," says my mom. "I'll have to drag you
guys with me now. Come on."

"No, no, no, we hate the grocery store! Please. Wait. Maybe I don't need a banana . . . I can use something else to call Mr. Nuggy." I grab the first thing I see. "Look, I can use dish soap!" I say.

"Okay, I guess I do need a banana," I say, and put the dish soap down.

"Get in the car," says my mom.

At the grocery store:

On line at the fish counter, my mom says, "Violet, you go get some yogurt; Luke, go choose a cereal; and Rascal, you . . ."

"Get bananas!" I say.

"Fine, then come right back," says my mom. "*And don't run.*"

I'm running down the freezer aisle and about to turn the corner when . . .

CRASH!

A grocery cart smacks me to the floor. And then the cart tries to flatten me.

"You're okay. Just shake it off, kid," says the lady who smashed me.

She reaches into her giant purse and searches around inside for a really long time. I hear lots of rattling around in there. A candy wrapper falls to the floor. Finally, she finds what she's looking for. A dollar bill.

"Here, take a dollar, and you'll forget all about your troubles." I stuff the dollar in my pocket and don't say a thing.

"Listen, since you're down there anyway, do me a favor, and reach that jar for me, hon?" she says. "These old knees don't want to bend."

"Thanks, kid," she says. "Nighty-night!" Then she wipes her forehead with a handkerchief. "Boy, it's hot in here."

This time I run even faster to the bananas.
I grab one and call Mr. Nuggy.

"Well, she's right here. At the grocery store.
No, she's not wearing her wings. . . . I think

they're too itchy. . . . It's definitely her. . . . She said 'Nighty-night.' Who else says 'nighty-night' in the afternoon?"

"She's buying a pineapple . . . nope . . . she just put it back."

"Warning! She's buying eggs—
she better not be planning on
cooking them."

Then my mom appears. "Rascal! There you
are! We've been looking everywhere for you.
Give me the bananas . . . all of them . . . and let's
go." I wave good-bye to the tooth fairy.

"Why are you waving to that woman?" asks
my mom, gripping my arm.

And then . . . I just have to. I want her to know what a good kid I really am. So across the lemons, I shout the only thing I can think of, "I WAS SO GOOD WHEN MY MOM GOT HER HAIR CUT! I LOVE YOU! *ALL* CHILDREN LOVE YOU!"

The tooth fairy looks uncertain. But then . . . her eyes begin to sparkle. And very slowly a smile spreads across her face. And her smile is GIGANTIC.

I feel my mom's fingers dig deeper into my arm. Then she grabs my hand and rushes us to the checkout line. Luke and Violet unload the cart faster than usual.

The tooth fairy is on the checkout line near us. When it's time for her to pay, she takes out a HUGE stack of one-dollar bills from her purse! And guess what she does when she sees me watching? *She winks at me!!!*

On the car ride home, I tell everybody, "I saw the tooth fairy at the grocery store."

"So *that's* what that was about," grumbles my mom.

"And she's definitely not going to give me eggs."

"Huh? Why would she give you eggs?"

"Ask Luke and Violet," I say.

"Um . . . we have no idea what she is talking about . . . as usual," says Violet.

"And look! She gave me a dollar!" I say.

"Where'd you get that?" asks my mom.

"I just told you! The tooth fairy!" I say, and wiggle my tooth with my tongue. It's so loose, it bends all the way back and forth.

CHAPTER 6
The Bulldog

"Guess what? I saw the tooth fairy at the grocery store!" I tell Rosabelle and George the next morning.

"She's all better?" asks Rosabelle.

"Yup, she's perfectly healthy and nice!"

"Really?" says George. "One time when I had a very high fever, I saw the Easter Bunny when we went through a car wash, but it wasn't the whole Easter Bunny, it was just a floating bunny head and—"

"Uh-oh," I say. "Look up!"

"Why is Mrs. Gobble Gracker wearing my dress-up clothes?" asks Rosabelle. "Those are my wings! That's my tutu! And my crown!"

"Look! She's got the tooth fairy's purse!" I say. "How did she get it?"

"I am the one and only tooth fairy now!" calls Mrs. Gobble Gracker. "The old tooth fairy is OUT! I captured her on her way home from the grocery store. She's a really slow driver."

Suddenly, this is a very big problem.

"Give me back my tutu!" yells Rosabelle.

"See you when you lose that tooth, Rascal! Sweet dreams!" yells Mrs. Gobble Gracker.

When we are safely inside, George says, "Whatever you do, don't wiggle your tooth."

"Let me see it," says Rosabelle. When I open my mouth she screams, "Rascal! Your tooth is hanging on by one string!"

one string

"Don't eat anything or it will fall out!" says George.

"And Mrs. Gobble Gracker will come to your room in the middle of the night!" says Rosabelle. "And steal your tooth!"

"And she definitely won't leave you any money," says George.

"I promise I won't eat," I tell them.

At morning meeting, my teacher takes the attendance. But Charlie, the attendance monitor, is absent. The teacher is going to pick a substitute attendance monitor. All my life, I have wanted to be the substitute attendance monitor (because I know she wouldn't pick me as the real attendance monitor).

"How about Dory?"

I skip down
the hallway.

But when I get to the office . . .

"Ridley! What are you doing here?" Ridley is Rosabelle's little brother.

"What are YOU doing here?" he asks.

"I'M the substitute attendance monitor."

"Well, I'm Batman. Want some candy?"

"You have candy?"

"Uh-huh. Gumdrops. I found them in my car seat." Ridley takes one out of his pocket.

"Why is it slimy?" I ask him.

"From the frog," he says.

I don't know what that means, but *candy is candy*. So I wipe off the slime with my shirt and take a bite.

I imagine I'm in the Gumdrop
Mountains....

Until I realize what happened when I took
that bite....

MY TOOTH FELL OUT!

"Mrs. Gobble Gracker is coming!" I gasp.

Then I run back to my classroom.

"Congratulations!" says my teacher. "Everybody, this is a such special moment, Dory just lost her first tooth."

"OH NO!" shrieks Rosabelle, and then quickly covers her mouth. The teacher gives Rosabelle a strange look. "Excuse me," says Rosabelle, embarrassed.

The teacher tells me to get a drink from the water fountain. When I come back, she gives me a yellow plastic necklace shaped like a tooth. My tooth rattles around inside.

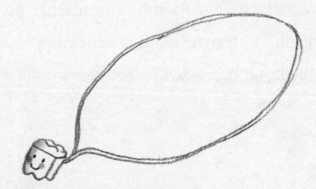

Then it's time to line up for gym.

"You need to be prepared for tonight," whispers Rosabelle.

"Make a trap for Mrs. Gobble Gracker," says George.

"And whatever you do, don't fall asleep!" says Rosabelle.

On the way home from school, I keep my mouth closed because I don't want Luke and Violet to notice that I lost a tooth. Just in case they start talking about *omelets* again. My tooth necklace is hidden safely in my pocket.

"Why isn't Dory talking?" asks Luke.

"I don't know, but it's totally freaking me out," says Violet

"Maybe she's dying," says Luke.

When I get home,
I hide my tooth in my
piggy bank.

Then I think about
how to cover up my gap.
I have an idea. "Have you seen my old vampire
teeth from Halloween?" I ask Mary.

"No," she says. But I can tell when she's lying.
So I look under the bed.

I found them!

The thing is, if you put vampire teeth in your mouth upside down, they're not vampire teeth anymore. They're bulldog teeth!

Vampire teeth

bulldog teeth

Then I gather a few supplies from around the house to make the trap for Mrs. Gobble Gracker. For some reason, no one notices when I take the toaster.

That night at dinner . . .

My mom sends me upstairs for time-out.

"Okay," I say. "But can I take the empty pizza box with me?"

"TAKE THE BOX!!" my mom yells at the top of her lungs. I don't know why.

At bedtime, my dad tucks me in. I'm lucky that it's my dad and not my mom because he doesn't notice I'm still wearing my bulldog teeth.

When he's gone, I sneak out of bed, grab my flashlight, and get my tooth out of my piggy bank. Then Mary and I set up the trap.

Setting up a trap takes a long time.

When we are done, we lie down on my sleeping bag. We try really hard to stay awake, but...

This is what was *supposed* to happen:

1. Mrs. Gobble Gracker tries to steal my tooth. But when she pulls on the string, toothpaste squirts into her eyes.

2. With toothpaste in her eyes, she trips on the dresser drawer on the floor.

3. When the drawer moves, it knocks off the bucket and the horsey from my dresser.

4. When the horsey falls, the toaster swings through the air and hits Mrs. Gobble Gracker in the head.

5. Mrs. Gobble Gracker falls into the box of LEGOs. When the LEGO box falls, my mattress crashes down from the ceiling and squashes her.

CHAPTER 7
Lost and Found

The next morning, I come downstairs crying. "Mrs. Gobble Gracker took my tooth last night. It's gone!"

"Did she take the toaster, too?" asks my dad.

"*What?* Rascal, your tooth *fell out?*" asks my mom. "Why didn't you tell us?"

"I tried to squash her with my mattress! But she's so sneaky, she got my tooth without setting off the trap!" I say, wiping my tears.

"Hey, Dad, can we have *omelets* for breakfast?" asks Luke. Then he smiles and winks at me.

"Don't worry," says my mom. "I'm sure we will find your tooth. It's probably in your room somewhere. So this would be a good day to clean your room."

"You don't want me to go to school?" I ask.

"It's Saturday," she says.

How does my mom always know when it's Saturday?

My mom helps me clean up the trap, but we still don't find the tooth.

I ask her if we can move to a new house so Mrs. Gobble Gracker can't find me.

"Not today," she says, "Melody is coming over."

"Melody! Again! Why?!" I say.

"Because I want to give her that beautiful

coat of yours. It's such a shame no one is wear-ing it, and I think it would be perfect for her."

"The bunchy coat?" I ask.

Ding-dong.

"Great! She's here already," says my mom.

When Melody tries on the coat, my mom gets very excited. "Oh! It's just adorable on you! I can't stand it!"

Melody does lots of smiley twirls.

"You look like a little snow queen," says my mom, hugging her. *Hey! She never said that to me.*

Melody does not want to take the coat off.

"Want to play Candy Land again, Rascal? The kind we played last time, remember? *Without the board?*" asks Melody. "Because look! I can be Queen Frostine! Queen of Frosting! And you can wear your goggles, like last time!"

"Okay! Sure," I say. "But first let's go on an adventure to get my tooth back."

"Back from where?" asks Melody.

"Mrs. Gobble Gracker took it," I say, putting on my goggles. "And she's up in the clouds, she thinks she's the tooth fairy."

"I'm not playing that," says Melody. "Definitely not. That's way too scary!"

"Are you sure?" I ask her. "Because we could get ALL the pillows in the house and put them on my bed. You know, for clouds. I promise it won't be scary… it will be soft and fluffy!"

"How about I organize your sock drawer instead?" Melody asks.

"Oh, fine."

I gather every pillow from around the house and stack them on my bed.

It's the tooth fairy! And she's saying a lot of really bad words. She thinks I'm Mrs. Gobble Gracker. Eeeek!

"Excuse me! Excuse me!" I say. "This isn't Mrs. Gobble Gracker! She must have lost your purse. And I found it! This is Dory . . . remember me? The *really good* kid from the grocery store! Where are you? . . . Locked in the top tower of the tooth castle? . . . The key is in this bag? Let me look for it. . . ."

The tooth fairy's purse is a mess. And of course, it's full of teeth.

GLITTER

FANCY BATHING CAP

CANDY

A LOT OF TEETH

EMPTY HOT SAUCE BOTTLE

DOLLARS

FLASHLIGHT

The World

MAP BOOK

At the bottom of her purse, I find the key. "I found it! Okay! I'm on my way!"

key

I run across a path of clouds to the tooth castle.

I climb the stairs to the top tower and un-lock the door.

"What took you so long? There are kids waiting for me all over the world," says the tooth fairy.

"And it's soooo hot in here," she says grabbing the purse from me. Even though she's a little grouchy, *I love her so much.*

"The first rule of being a tooth fairy is hold on to your purse! Mrs. Gobble Gracker sure has a lot to learn," says the tooth fairy.

"How are we going to stop her?" I ask.

"Give me a minute," she says. "I'll make her a present."

"A *present?*" I say.

"Trust me," she says, and gives me a wink.

Just then Melody walks up the tower stairs.

"Queen Frostine! What are you doing here?"

"What a beautiful coat!" says the tooth fairy.

"Look! I found your tooth!" says Melody. "It was in your sock drawer."

"Sock drawer? How
did it get there?"

"And here's a bunch of socks
with no match! What should I do
with them?" asks Melody.

"Can you just hold on to those?" I ask.

"Okay, but can we play Candy Land now?" she asks.

"One second," I say. "I'm almost done here."

"All set!" says the tooth fairy putting on her wings. "I have to make a quick call to my husband before I go," she says. "Just so he knows I'm safe."

"Okay, here's the present for Mrs. Gobble Gracker," says the tooth fairy, handing it to us.

Help!

"Dory, put that tooth under your pillow tonight!" she says as we follow her downstairs.

"Nighty-night," she says, and flies away.

Mrs. Gobble Gracker lands her plane right outside the castle.

"We have a present for you," I say.

"A present! For me?" she asks.

She opens the box.

That night, I put my tooth under my pillow. I'm so tired from my adventure that I fall asleep right away.

In the morning when I wake up, I check under my pillow. My tooth is gone. And there's a dollar. And a lollipop.

Before I jump out of bed and tell my family the good news, I think of the Lollipop Forest.

One lick and I'm gone.

There's hidden treasure
in the next adventure about

DORY
FANTASMaGory

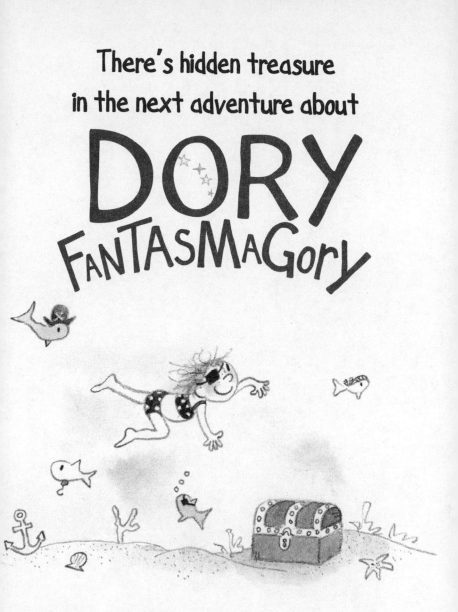

Turn the page for a sneak peek!

CHAPTER 1
Such an Amazing Bath Toy

My name is Dory but everyone calls me Rascal. I have a big sister named Violet and a big brother named Luke. They have a lot of activities after school. But not me. Because I like to go home and make up my own activities. But today I'm going to the library with my mom. "I love our afternoons together," says my mom. "You're my little partner."

1

I return my books to the librarian so I can check out new ones. But first, I need to talk to her. "Excuse me. I'm trying to find that book about a family who eats breakfast in the shower and the mom wears a dress that's made out of live chickens . . ." I ask her.

"And the boy eats with his
feet and the dad thinks that's
really good manners. The dad
says, 'By golly!' And then the
lights go off and they think
they're dead but then their cat
and dog turn on the electricity."

"Rascal, are you making
this up?" asks my mom.

"No! It's a real book. And
then they think they're in
heaven! But they're really
in their living room! It's so
funny! And then they
wear sneakers to bed!
Do you have that
book?"

"I'm sorry, I don't know that one," says the librarian. "But here's a series you might like, it's called Happy Little Farm."

"That's okay. Thanks anyway," says my mom. She leads me away from the desk and whispers, "Stop growling."

My mom finds some books she likes and reads to me. After seven books she says, "Rascal, I'm going to the bathroom. I want you to read quietly while I'm gone, okay?"

"I can't read."

"Yes, you can," she says. "I'll be right back."

Suddenly, a very short kid wearing a dinosaur tail is standing close to me. Her voice sounds like a frog. "Wead me it," she says pointing to her book.

"I'm a bad reader," I whisper.

"Wead it!" she says.

"Ask someone else," I say.

"I weally want you," says the kid.

"I could tell you a story instead," I suggest.

"I want a scawy story," she says.

"Well, that's easy. . . . Once upon a time . . ."
I whisper, "well, actually right
now, there lives a
robber named
Mrs. Gobble
Gracker."

"Mrs. Wobba Wacka?"

"Yes . . . and she's very sneaky. . . . She lives in a cave and she is 507 years old and has a big black cape . . . and . . . and . . . she has really long fingernails and FANGS like this . . . and she's been looking for me for a long time. I'm in great danger. She wants to drag me off to her cave and pretend I'm her baby."

"I want to be in danger," she says.

"Me too," says another kid.

"Are you scared?" asks a third kid.

"Of course I'm scared! But I have a monster and a fairy godmother who help me fight Mrs. Gobble Gracker. My monster sleeps under my bed. Her name is Mary. She is my best friend. And my fairy godmother is named Mr. Nuggy, and he can do magic. He lives in the trees and he

7

has a big mustache, and once, a long time ago, he turned into a chicken. If I have an emergency, I can call him for help. I can call him from a banana."

"Boy, these kids have a lot of questions!"

Before I can answer, the girl with the dinosaur tail tells everyone to be quiet. "Shhhh! Mrs. Wobba Wacka woke up!" she says. "She was asleep inside the earth."

"What are you talking about? She sleeps in her cave!" I say. "And it's far away."

"She woke up and she wants bweakfast!" she says.

"How do you know?" I say.

"Quick we gotta make it!" says another kid. Then all the kids start making breakfast no matter what I say.

"If we don't make it faster, she'll throw bones at us," says one kid.

"I just saw a flying bone!" says another kid. "That means she's getting closer!"

"Oh no!" says the littlest kid, diving into the couch.

"Just so you know," I tell them, "Mrs. Gobble Gracker drinks coffee in the morning. She loves coffee."

"NO! She drinks *sauce*! Not coffee!" says a little boy.

"Uh-oh," I say. "Here she comes."

"Dory—say good-bye. We're leaving," says my mom, trying to get away from the little kids.

"But I didn't check out any books!" I say.

"I know, but I asked you to read quietly," she says. "And instead you've made all these kids crazy."

"They were born that way!"

My mom apologizes to the librarian as we head toward the door.

On the way home, my mom says, "Rascal, I was thinking, well, you know how you out-grow things when you get older, like your shoes? Well, you might outgrow *other things* too, like your Mrs. Gobble Gracker game, for example."

"I'm not outgrowing them," I say. "My shoes are shrinking."

"No, they're not," says my mom.

"Yes, they are!" I say.

"No, they're not," says my mom.

"Yes, they are!"

"Okay, I have an idea. What if we got you a new toy, *something really special*. Something that you might play with a lot, that might be even more fun than your Mrs. Gobble Gracker game."

"Like a bribe?" I say.

"Wha—no, Rascal! No!"

"Okay, I know what I want."

My mom looks happy. "What is it, honey?" she asks.

"TUBTOWN! I saw a picture of it in an old magazine at Grandma's house. It's a town that sticks to the bathtub.

"It has suction cups that make it stick! It has an elevator! And a shower! And a fish-and-chips shop, and a lighthouse, and a pool with a diving board, and a little raft that the people can go in and float around the bathtub and—"

"Rascal, we already talked about this. That was a very old magazine. They don't make that toy anymore. I can't buy it."

"But that's impossible! Why would they stop making *the best toy in the world*?"

"They just did," says my mom. "I already tried to get it. It doesn't exist anymore."

"Does this have something to do with pirates?" I ask my mom.

"I don't think so," she says. "I have an idea. How about we get you a magic set?"

16

"I already have magic," I say.

"Come on! I need to take a bath right away!"

When I'm in the tub, Violet gets home from her dance class.